little Miss Fickle

by Roger Hargreaves

Would you like me to tell you a story?

If you were Little Miss Fickle,
you'd say, "Yes, please!"
And then you'd say, "No, thank you!"
And then you'd say, "Yes!" again.

Little Miss Fickle was one of those people
who just could not make up their minds.

Ever!

About anything!

Little Miss Fickle lived in Dandelion Cottage which was on the outskirts of Sunnytown.

And she lived right next door to her best friend, Little Miss Neat, who lived in Twopin Cottage.

One Monday, Little Miss Fickle and
Little Miss Neat went out to lunch in Sunnytown.

"I'll have the soup to start with," said
Little Miss Neat to the waiter as she looked
at the menu, "followed by the fish."

"So will I," said Little Miss Fickle.

But after the waiter had written down the order,
Little Miss Fickle looked at the menu again.

"No I won't," she said. "I'll have the salad instead,
followed by the roast chicken!"

The waiter crossed out the first order, and
wrote down the second.

"On the other hand," continued Little Miss Fickle,
"I won't have anything to start with...
but then I'll have the eggs!"

The waiter sighed.

An hour later, after the waiter had worn out three pencils and four order pads, Little Miss Fickle finally made up her mind to have the soup, followed by the fish.

The waiter brought the soup.

Little Miss Fickle looked at it.
"I'm not hungry any more," she said.

It was at that moment that the waiter decided he was going to be a bus conductor instead of a waiter.

On Tuesday, Little Miss Fickle went to
buy a hat.

"I want a new pink hat," she announced to
the milliner.

The milliner brought her two pink hats
to choose from.

"I'll have this one," said Little Miss Fickle, after
she had tried them both on.

"Certainly, Madam," replied the milliner,
and put the hat in a hatbox.

"On the other hand," said Little Miss Fickle,
"I think I'll have the other hat!"

The milliner took the first hat out of the hatbox...
and then put the second hat into the hatbox!

"But," continued Little Miss Fickle, "I think the
first hat suited me better, don't you?"

The milliner didn't say a word as she took the
second hat out of the hatbox...
and then put the first hat back into the hatbox!

She handed the hatbox to Little Miss Fickle.

Little Miss Fickle looked at the milliner.

"Do you have any blue hats?" she asked.

It was at that moment that the milliner decided she was going to be a ballerina instead of a milliner!

On Wednesday, Little Miss Fickle went to the butcher's.

"I'd like some sausages," she said.

"Beef sausages, or pork sausages?" asked the butcher.

"Pork sausages," replied Little Miss Fickle.

The butcher wrapped up the pork sausages.

"But beef sausages would be nicer," said
Little Miss Fickle.

The butcher unwrapped the pork sausages,
and wrapped up some beef sausages instead.

"On the other hand," continued Little Miss Fickle,
"chops would be tastier!"

It was at that moment that the butcher
decided he needed a holiday.

But, on Thursday, guess what happened?
Little Miss Fickle disappeared!
Little Miss Neat had seen her pass Twopin Cottage
on the way into Sunnytown, but she hadn't come back.

She didn't come back on Friday, either.
So Little Miss Neat went looking for her.

She met Mr Muddle.
"Have you seen Little Miss Fickle?" she
asked anxiously.
Mr Muddle looked at her in a puzzled sort of a way.
"Did you say, 'Have I been for a little tickle?' " he asked.
"Oh, Mr Muddle," said Little Miss Neat, and hurried on.

Then Little Miss Neat met Mr Forgetful.

"Have you seen Little Miss Fickle?" she asked.
Mr Forgetful thought.

"Well," she said, "have you?"
Mr Forgetful thought again.

"Have I what?" he asked, after a while.
"Oh, Mr Forgetful," said Little Miss Neat,
and hurried on.

But could she find Little Miss Fickle?
No, she could not!
Nobody had seen her.

The Sunnytown Public Lending Library has...
nineteen thousand,
nine hundred,
and ninety-nine books.

On Saturday afternoon, Little Miss Fickle reached up
and took one of them down from a shelf.

"I'll read this one," she thought to herself.

"On the other hand," she thought again, looking at
another book, "perhaps I'll read that book instead!"

She put the first book back on the shelf,
and took the other book down.

It was the nineteen thousand,
nine hundred,
and ninety-ninth book she had chosen!

Little Miss Fickle had been in the library for three
days choosing a book.

Three whole days choosing just one single,
solitary book!

She went home carrying her book.

That Saturday afternoon, Little Miss Neat was in the garden of Twopin Cottage when Little Miss Fickle walked past.

"Where have you BEEN?" she called out.

"To the library," replied Little Miss Fickle.

"For THREE days?" exclaimed Little Miss Neat.

"Well," explained Little Miss Fickle,
"I wanted to choose the right book!"

And she held it up.
And then she stopped and looked at it.

"Oh, botherations!" she said.
"I've read it before!"

Fantastic offers for Little Miss fans!

cut along the dotted line and return this whole page

Only need a few Little Miss or Mr. Men to complete your set? You can order any of the titles on the back of the books from our Mr. Men order line on 0870 787 1724. Orders should be delivered between 5 and 7 working days.

--- TO BE COMPLETED BY AN ADULT ---

To apply for any of these great offers, ask an adult to complete the details below and send this whole page with the appropriate payment and tokens, to: MR. MEN CLASSIC OFFER, PO BOX 715, HORSHAM RH12 5WG

☐ Please send me a giant-sized double-sided collectors' poster.

AND ☐ I enclose 6 tokens and have taped a £1 coin to the other side of this page.

☐ Please send me ☐ Mr. Men Library case(s) and/or ☐ Little Miss library case(s) at £5.99 each inc P&P

☐ I enclose a cheque/postal order payable to Egmont UK Limited for £..........

OR ☐ Please debit my MasterCard / Visa / Maestro / Delta account (delete as appropriate) for £..........

Card no. ☐☐☐☐ ☐☐☐☐ ☐☐☐☐ ☐☐☐☐ ☐☐☐☐   Security code ☐☐☐

Issue no. (if available) ☐   Start Date ☐☐/☐☐/☐☐   Expiry Date ☐☐/☐☐/☐☐

Fan's name: .... Date of birth: ....

Address: ....

....

Postcode: ....

Name of parent / guardian: ....

Email for parent / guardian: ....

Signature of parent / guardian: ....

Please allow 28 days for delivery. Offer is only available while stocks last. We reserve the right to change the terms of this offer at any time and we offer a 14 day money back guarantee. This does not affect your statutory rights. Offers apply to UK only.

☐ We may occasionally wish to send you information about other Egmont children's books. If you would rather we didn't, please tick this box.

Ref: LIM 001

cut along the dotted line and return this whole page